THE STICK MAN WITH A BIG BUM

and the MASSIVE Surprise

Eric (the Stick Man) Trum
Jonny Staples

'It's not that I'm so smart,

it's just that I stay with problems longer.'

-Einstein

Hello there, I'm Eric Trum and this is a picture of me.

Yes, I have carefully hidden my bum in this picture as I am rather embarrassed about it. Over the last month I've found a few good hiding places for it. Here are a few of them.

not my best idea

glue

hiding it in a
bunch of grapes

popped it in a
hole in a log
(stuck for 2 days)

Clever hey?

Those of you who've read my other books will already know the rule…. 'Don't look at my bum.'

And for those of you who are new, turn the page for a little reminder poster….

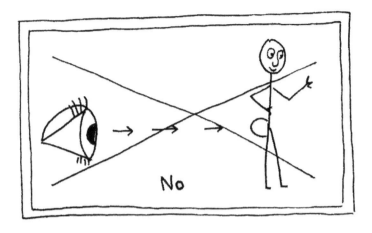

Good, I'm glad that's sorted.

Just in case you don't know, I was drawn by Jonny Staples nearly one year ago. He was rather surprised when I came alive and we've been living together ever since.

Now this story begins on the day the postman knocked on the door of our house, 41 Brooklands Avenue. When Jonny answered it he was amazed to be handed a beautifully wrapped box.

'Open it, open it,' I shouted while jumping up as high as I could, (which isn't very high as my bum sort of weighs me down.) Jonny looked at the gift tag and read it out…

'For Jonny and Eric, open on Eric's birthday.'

I couldn't believe it; my birthday wasn't for another two days. I lay down and punched the carpet for at least a minute.

'You have to learn to wait for things,' said Jonny, placing the parcel on top of the fridge. I grumbled for a while but tried not to complain.

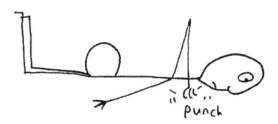

I decided I needed to take my mind off that box so I climbed onto Jonny's shoulder. 'We need some new activities to do,' I said. While I was up there I saw a pile of inflated balloons hidden behind a table.

'Balloons,' I shouted, sliding down his arm and running into the pile.

'Well I was saving those for your birthday,' said Jonny, 'but I do know a good activity we could do with them right now.'

'Oh, what is it? I asked.

Activity Number 1

Balloon Collector

'It's called the balloon collector,' said Jonny. He got about fifteen of the inflated balloons out and put them on the carpet. 'The game is to see who can hold the most number of balloons at once, shall I go first?' I nodded and sat on the arm of the sofa to watch.

Jonny started tucking the knots of the balloons into his button holes, pushing some of the balloons between his knees and under his arms, he even got one under his chin. I counted them up... he was holding **10 balloons!**

After he'd released them he wrote the number ten in his notebook. 'Right Eric, your go,' he said. I stood in the middle of the balloons and tried to put one between my knees but it was far too big and ended up holding me up which wasn't quite the idea of the game.

In the end I managed to hold one above my head like this.

Jonny wrote down the number one. 'Well it looks like I'm the winner', he said smiling.

'I'm not sure it's fair,' I said, 'so I've got an idea for a different game.' I took one of the non-inflated balloons from the packet I'd found by the TV and started climbing inside.

'How many balloons can you sit inside?' I said sitting down, 'I can do one.' Jonny wrote **'one'** in his notebook before trying to climb into one of the other balloons. He got his big toe in but that was all.

I think I won that game, I said. I tried to get out of the balloon but found that my bum was stuck!

The balloon was attached to me for the rest of the day. It was **extremely** embarrassing! Jonny eventually managed to remove the balloon using nail clippers. (It was a very nerve racking time.)

Once I was free Jonny put the balloons around the house ready for my birthday. They looked pretty good.

I didn't sleep well that night. I was just sooooooo excited about what was in that box. I lay in my little margarine tub bed and wondered what on earth it could be.

Over breakfast Jonny told me he planned to invite our neighbour Jeremy Mothballs round for my birthday tea. We decided it would be nice to make him a very special invitation.

Activity Number 2

Hide the Clue Game

We wrote out the invitation and I even drew some balloons on it.

'Let's make a game where he has to find the invitation,' said Jonny, 'he'll love it.'

'How do we do it?' I asked.

'Well we need to make clues that lead to it.'

'But he might not find it and then he won't come,' I said scratching my head.

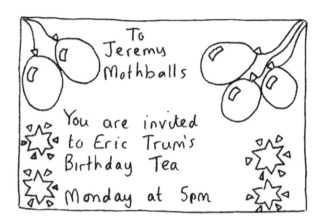

To
Jeremy
Mothballs

You are invited
to Eric Trum's
Birthday Tea
Monday at 5pm

Jonny promised that everything would be okay

'Now for the fun bit,' said Jonny. He wrote the first clue, which said…

There's a special message for you, look under the swing in the park

We posted that clue through Jeremy Mothball's door and ran to the park, I was in Jonny's pocket and it was really fun jiggling up and down. When we got there, we taped the second clue to the underneath of one of the swings. The second clue said…

Look behind the parsnips at Ruby's vegetable shop.

We ran to Ruby's and tucked the third clue under the parsnips. The third clue said…

Check out the cookery books at the library.

We hid the next clue between two cookery books, it said…

Look under the plant pot in your garden.

We ran to Jeremy's garden and put the actual invitation under the big blue plant pot that sits by his front door.

After that we rushed home giggling.

TOP TIP

The hide the clue game isn't just for invitations, you can also play it around your house, just have a prize or a well-done message at the end. You need to hide clues, each one leading to the next one. Just tell the other person where the first clue is to start them off. Here are a few ideas for good hiding places….

your spoon drawer

underneath a table

in a toilet roll

blue tacked to the top of a door frame

MY BIRTHDAY

I woke at 5am on my birthday morning. I tried to wake Jonny by sitting on his nose but it wasn't working so I sat in the kitchen and looked at the box on top of the fridge. I was there for two hours.

Eventually Jonny got up and ambled through. He got my breakfast, which was one shreddie, and then, **FINALLY**, he got the box down and put it on the table.

'I wonder who it's from,' he said looking at the tag, 'it says open on Eric's birthday and that's today so..... let's open it.'

We started tearing the paper off until we were left with a brown cardboard box. It was strange because there were small holes punched in the side. Jonny pulled the tape off the top and together we opened it and peered in.

'Hello,' said a tiny voice from inside.

We looked at each other and everything went quiet. Jonny reached into the box and carefully lifted out the contents. It was another stick man! A little man, about the same size as me climbed onto Jonny's hand.

He looked at Jonny, jumped off his hand and brushed himself down. 'Ewww I shouldn't have touched a human,' he said. He looked at me, 'are you a stick man too?' he asked.

I nodded, 'yes.'

'I've never seen another stick man before,' he said.

'Well I'm Eric Trum, who are you?'

'I don't really have a name,' he said.

'So where are you from?' I asked.

'I was drawn on a piece of paper by a man in a purple cardigan. A few minutes later I came alive. When the man saw me moving around he freaked out and threw me behind his kitchen bin where I've been living ever since.'

'Who is this man?' asked Jonny.

'I don't know, but every time he looked at me he clutched his head and said I couldn't be real. He said that humans and stick men weren't meant to exist together.'

Jonny and I looked at each other.

'So how did you end up here?' I said.

'One day the man said he was going on holiday so there would be no rubbish for me to eat. He put me in a box and that's the last thing I remember.'

Bob suddenly saw my bottom and couldn't stop staring, 'is that a grape?' he asked.

I moved so my bum so it was hidden behind a box

of cereal.

'Um, no,' I said, going red.

'So,' said Jonny, trying to change the subject, 'how come you don't have a name?'

'I was never given one, can you help me think of one?'

We discussed various possibilities and came up with the name Bob. Bob was very pleased and I saw a smile spread across his face.

'Well Bob, my name's Jonny.' He went to shake Bob's hand but Bob said he'd rather not touch a human.

We spent the morning showing Bob around the house and telling him about all the different activities we'd done. He asked me about my bum again but I said I'd banged my hip and it was just a bump like you might have on your head. After that I started walking like this to make it less obvious.

Bob was very impressed with my margarine tub

bed. 'I would love something like that,' he said.

'I'll make you one,' said Jonny.

Bob said he'd like his bed to be put behind the bin because that was what he was used to. He also said that I should sleep in the kitchen with him, as a human and a stick man shouldn't share a room.

I was horrified, there was no way I was sleeping behind the smelly bin. I liked my little tub bed in a shoe box next to the radiator in Jonny's room.

Bob and I sat on the sofa for the rest of the morning and watched Tim's Toys on YouTube. Later there was a knock on the door. It was our neighbour Jeremy Mothballs, holding all the clues in his hand.

'Good clues,' he said beaming.

We welcomed him in and introduced him to Bob. 'Nice to meet you,' said Jeremy.

Bob started laughing, 'haha,' he said, 'why have you got such a ridiculous moustache? Is it a joke?' He pointed at Jeremy's face.

Jeremy looked at us.

'Um why don't you go and get a Shreddie from the kitchen?' said Jonny. Bob went through to the kitchen, still laughing.

'I can't believe there's another stick man,' whispered Jeremy, 'where's he from?'

Jonny told Jeremy all about the mysterious box. 'Wow,' said Jeremy, his mouth hanging open.

Activity Number 3

Hunt the Thimble

'Shall we play a game of hunt the thimble before the party tea?' asked Jonny. Me and Jeremy nodded and Jonny got a thimble out of his pocket. 'I'll be the hider first,' he said.

How to play

1. Take a thimble or other small object.
2. Decide who it going to be the hider
3. Everyone except the hider leaves the room
4. The hider has to put the thimble somewhere where it can be seen but is not obvious, (so no pushing it under a cushion or anything.)
5. The others come back in and look for the thimble. (If they're struggling the hider can shout hot, warm or cold depending on how near they are to it.)
6. The winner is the first person to find it.

How it went for us

We went into the kitchen to wait while Jonny hid the thimble and noticed that Bob had fallen asleep amongst a bunch of grapes.

After a couple of minutes, we heard Jonny shout

'ready,' from the lounge.

Leaving Bob to have his nap, Jeremy and I ran through and started looking everywhere. We looked for ages before Jonny agreed to help us. He shouted 'warm' when we were by the coffee table, which meant that we were quite near. I jumped up into the fruit bowl and he shouted 'hot.' In the end I found it neatly tucked onto the end of a banana.

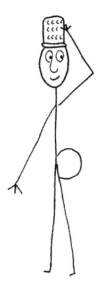

'Clever hiding place,' I said, grabbing the thimble

and balancing it on my head.

Next I hid it on a lamp. It took them ages to find because it looked like a switch then Jeremy hid it on his nose which we both got straight away.

'What a good game I said,' filling the thimble up with apple juice and having a drink. After that we played keep the balloon in the air where we all had to leap about making sure a balloon didn't touch the ground for twenty minutes.

'I think it's time for that party tea now', said Jonny once we were all tired of the game.

Activity Number 4

Wacky Sandwiches

'Hello there,' said Bob as we went back into the kitchen. He rolled off the grapes and onto the table.

'Hi Bob,' said Jonny, 'would you like to have some Birthday snacks?' Bob nodded and stood up. I sat in an egg cup, (perfect bum hiding place), while Jonny got four plates of sandwiches out of the cupboard.

The sandwiches were small and square and I immediately ran up to have a closer look. I took a tiny

bite out of one of them and this is what I looked like....

'What's in it?' I asked, my eyes nearly falling out of my head.

'Well that one is a mixture of crisps and chocolate buttons,' said Jonny.

Bob took a bite of a sandwich on a different plate, 'quite nice,' he said, 'just like food from the bin.'

'That sandwich is made with mini marshmallows and ketchup,' said Jonny. Bob smiled, 'I love it,' he said, finishing it off.

Jeremy took a sandwich from the third plate. 'He looked confuzzed (mixture of confused and puzzled) before smiling, 'surprisingly delicious,' he said, 'is it banana and marmite?'

Jonny nodded and tucked into a banana and marmite sandwich himself.

It was really fun trying to guess the ingredients. My favourite was on plate four, Nutella and chicken.

How to make them

The idea of wacky sandwiches is to have fillings that you wouldn't normally eat together. Something sweet and something savoury works well.

Here are a few more ideas

Chocolate and cheese

Anchovy and jelly babies

Fried egg and cornflakes

Hard-boiled egg and jam

Make sure the sandwiches are small and have a bucket ready just in case someone wants to spit one out.

You could even blindfold people to make the surprise even bigger.

After the sandwiches, Jonny got the pudding out and everyone sang happy birthday. The pudding was spaghetti hoops in jelly which was actually rather nice.

'Hey,' Jeremy said as he was leaving, 'we've not had a conundrums night for a while, shall we have one on Saturday at my house?'

'Yes,' Jonny and I said at the same time.

'what's a conundrum?' asked Bob.

'Well,' said Jonny, 'it's like a puzzle where we take it in turns to ask questions and the answer is always something unexpected.'

Bob looked very confused but said he would come

too.

Bob settled in over the next few days. He didn't tend to eat with us though, he preferred to sit in his margarine tub behind the bin and eat scraps. It was all going well until Thursday.

I was just researching something when Bob ran through into the lounge. He looked at me and said, 'Eric, that bump on your bottom doesn't seem to be going down.' I froze, unable to think of a single thing to say. 'It's not a bump is it... it's your bum,' he continued, before rolling around on the floor laughing.

'It is a bump,' I said going bright red.

'A bump without the letter P,' Bob said jumping from one leg to the other.

I looked at my book and pretended to read, eventually he went back into the kitchen. When I saw him later he acted like nothing had happened.

Activity Number 5

Conundrum Party

On Saturday we all went around to Jeremy's carrying our conundrum questions. Even Bob had done some.

'Come in, come in,' said Jeremy showing us all through to his lounge. He'd made popcorn and we sat on the sofa tucking in.

'Right Eric,' said Jeremy, you go first. I nodded and went to stand on the little wooden stage. I read out my

5 conundrums. Here they are. See if you can work them out. (The answers will be coming in a few pages.)

QUESTIONS

<u>Eric's Conundrums</u>

1. *How many beans can you put into an empty box?*
2. *If you had five parsnips and had to share them equally between three people, how would you do it?*
3. *Why can't a man living in Australia be buried in America?*
4. *What has 100 limbs but cannot walk?*
5. *How do you make the number ONE disappear?*

Jonny and Jeremy were busy writing down their answers. Bob just wrote down one answer.

'You have to try and guess all of them,' said Jonny.

'But you already told me the answer,' said Bob.

'What are you talking about?' said Jonny.

The other day you said that the answer to a conundrum is always 'something unexpected' so I've just written that down.

We all looked at each other in confuzzlement then carried on.

Jonny got up and read out his.

Jonny's conundrums

1. What has a neck but no head?
2. What increases its value by being turned upside down?
3. What kind of coat has no sleeves, no pockets, no buttons and won't keep you warm?
4. Who can shave 20 times a day and still have a beard?
5. What tastes better than it smells?

These are tricky I said, scratching my head. I tried to ride my pencil hoping that would help me to think but it didn't.

I guessed a few, well I guessed that a skunk tastes better than it smells but that was about it.

Jeremy jumped up next, he was wearing his parsnip costume, (just for fun).

Jeremy's conundrums

1. *What turns everything around without moving?*
2. *What loses its head in the morning but gets it back at night.*
3. *What table can you eat?*
4. *What is brown and sticky?*
5. *When you're given one you immediately have two or more. What is it?*

Right, said Jeremy once we'd all stopped writing, it's Bob's go.

Bob looked up. 'I've only got two questions,' he said, 'and they've both got the same answer.'

'That's okay,' said Jeremy.

Bob stood up and asked his two questions which were....

Bob's conundrums

1. *What do you get if you stick your head in a hole marked 'danger, an unknown thing is in this hole?'*
2. *What do you get if you put a gummy worm down a policeman's trousers?'*

Bob sat down and we all tried to think of answers. Bob suddenly stood up, 'I just want to say that I was told that the answer had to be 'something unexpected' so I spent hours thinking of questions with that answer.'

'You mean the answers to both your conundrums are just 'something unexpected?'' said Jonny.

Bob nodded.

Jonny started laughing which annoyed Bob and I just looked confused then we went through all the other answers…

ANSWERS

Eric's answers

1. *How many beans can you put into an empty box?* **One, after that it is not empty**
2. *If you had five potatoes and had to share them equally between three people, how would you do it?* **Mash and weigh**
3. *Why can't a man living in Australia be buried in America?* **Because he's not dead**
4. *What has 100 limbs but cannot walk?* **A tree**
5. *How do you make the number ONE disappear?* **Add the letter G and it's GONE**

Jonny's answers

1. *What has a neck but no head?* **A bottle**
2. *What increases its value by being turned upside down?* **The number 6**
3. *What kind of coat has no sleeves, no pockets, no buttons and won't keep you warm?* **A coat of paint**
4. *Who can shave 20 times a day and still have a beard?* **A barber**

5. *What tastes better than it smells?* **A tongue**

Jeremy's answers

1. *What turns everything around without moving?* ***A mirror***
2. *What loses its head in the morning but gets it back at night?* ***A pillow***
3. *What table can you eat?* ***A vegetable***
4. *What is brown and sticky?* ***A stick***
5. *When you're given one you immediately have two or more. What is it?* ***A choice*** *(good one Jeremy)*

Bob's answers

1. *What do you get if you stick you head in a hole marked 'danger, unknown thing is in this hole?'* ***Something unexpected***
2. *What do you get if you put a gummy worm down a policeman's trousers?'* ***Something unexpected***

After reading the answers we added up our

scores….

Jonny =4

Jeremy = 2

Eric = 1

Bob = 0

Jonny was dancing all around the room singing some song about being the winner.

I was a bit upset that I'd done so badly. The only point I got was for my guess of skunk and that wasn't even the official answer. Oh well, at least I beat Bob.

'You cheated by telling me the wrong answer,' Bob said to Jonny. 'You said the answer to a conundrum was 'something unexpected' and that wasn't that answer to any of them. I hate humans,' he shouted before rolling under a pillow and hiding. I had no idea what he was talking about so I just hid my bottom under a blanket and stared straight ahead.

Bob was soon lured out by Jeremy's delicious baked bananas though. They were amazing and Jonny asked for the recipe so we could try making them at home.

Activity Number 6

Baked Bananas

Ingredients

One ripe banana per person

A bag of chocolate buttons

vanilla ice cream to add at the end

Method

Put the oven on to 180c/gas mark 6

Slit through the skin of the bananas down the length of the inside.

Poke chocolate buttons along the cut.

Wrap each banana in tin foil.

Put onto a baking tray and place in the oven for 25 minutes.

Once ready, add some ice cream and eat the bananas straight from the skin.

They were **YUMPOLISCIOUS** although I got a little messy while eating mine and had to have a shower under a tap afterwards.

We thanked Jeremy for a great evening and walked home. Bob was mumbling about how he was tricked all the way back.

I woke early the next day and went into the kitchen to find Bob sitting on the edge of the bin eating an egg shell.

'You really should move into the kitchen with me,' he said, 'you know stick men and humans shouldn't be together.'

'Um, I'll think about it,' I said, knowing that there was no way I was moving.

I'd just finished my cheerio breakfast when Jonny came in. Bob immediately started laughing, 'haha look at you,' he said, pointing at Jonny's favourite silk dressing gown.

'Well I like Jonny's dressing gown,' I said.

Jonny got himself some toast and asked if we'd like to have a go at making drinking straw rockets.

'Yes please,' I said.

'What's a drinking straw rocket?' said Bob.

We all sat at the kitchen table and Jonny explained.

ACTIVITY NUMBER 7

Drinking Straw Rockets

Equipment needed

One bendy drinking straw per person

A pencil

Paper

Scissors

Sellotape (scotch tape)

(you may want to wear goggles just in case)

Jonny got the equipment out of a bag and placed it on the table. Bob and I immediately started talking to each other down the straw. Me at one end and him at the other. It worked pretty well as a telephone.

'Right,' said Jonny, let's start making our rockets.

Method

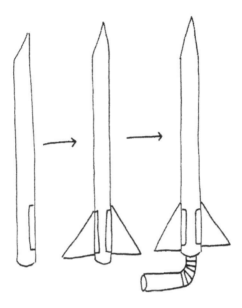

Cut a piece of paper that is about 12cm by 4cm per person. Roll this around the pencil and sellotape the edge to make your basic rocket shape. Remove the pencil..

Fold over one end of the tube to make a pointy tip and tape into place. Make sure there are no gaps for air to escape.

Cut out two sets of fins and sellotape them near the open end of the tube…. Your rocket is now made!

Once our rockets were ready we ran around with them. Bob threw his off the table and it dropped onto the ground.

'It didn't work,' he said, looking at it lying on the floor.

'Well that's why we need the straw,' said Jonny. He picked up Bob's rocket and put one of the bendy straws inside it. He took a big breath, blew into the straw and the rocket shot up into the air. Bob clapped his hands as he looked up in amazement.

'I want a go,' I said. Jonny helped me set it up and I did the biggest blow I've ever done....

Even though my eyes went funny it was worth it because mine went so high it actually hit the ceiling.

We had a lot of fun playing with our straw rockets and had a competition outside to see who could make theirs go the highest. Jonny won, but that was because we were standing up and he's the tallest so his rocket was starting from a much higher place. That didn't stop him celebrating though.

Jonny was about to have one last blow when Bob ran up his body, along his arm and jumped onto the rocket just as Jonny blew......

He flew up into the air. I covered my mouth in shock as I saw him fly away. The rocket landed high up in a tree.

'Help, help,' shouted Bob from the branches.

It took Jonny quite a long time to help Bob down as he had to go and borrow a ladder from his friend Firna Rex Shaw who lives down the road.

'I can't believe you threw me into that tree,' said Bob once we were all safely back in the kitchen. 'I told you humans were bad,' he added to me.

'But you jumped onto the rocket,' I said.

'That's not the point,' said Bob looking cross.

Straw Rockets Science Bit (Thank you Jonny)

When you blow into the straw, air it travels to the end and pushes its way out, taking the rocket with it as it moves. The harder you blow the more energy the air has and the further your rocket will fly!

That night we had a go at making a computer game on Scratch which was quite fun then it was time to go to bed.

'Move your tub into the kitchen tonight Eric,' said

Bob.

'I'm fine thanks,' I said, rushing upstairs.

'Why doesn't Bob like humans?' I asked once me and Jonny were in our room.

'Perhaps because the human he lived with wasn't kind to him?' said Bob.

'But that doesn't mean all humans are bad,' I said as I tucked myself into my sleeping sock.

A postcard arrived at 41 Brooklands Avenue (our house) the next day. Jonny spent a long time reading it.

'Who is Ludwig Meddler?' asked Jonny eventually.

'Um that'll be me,' said Bob rushing over for a look.

'I thought you didn't have a name?' I said.

'Well I do, but I prefer Bob,' said Bob.

'What does it say?' I asked.

Jonny read the postcard out.

'Dear Jonny, you may have received a parcel containing a stick man. I think he's just a doodle, but just in case he's alive thank you for looking after him.

I am on an island called Ibiza. It is good but a bit hot. I have been surfing and I went to the market where I bought a new purple cardigan. I will collect Ludwig in two weeks. I have missed him and can't wait to have him back.'

Best wishes

Keith Kettle-Chaser'

Bob dropped to the floor.

'I don't want to be collected in two weeks,' he said, 'I want to live here forever. I don't even like Keith Kettle-Chaser and he doesn't like me.'

After that Bob ran out into the garden and Jonny and I spent most of the morning looking for him.

Quite a long time later I found him crouched under a flower.

'Come back in,' I said, 'I'll make you a thimbleful of tea.'

'No, I like to be around plants when I'm upset,' he said. I went back inside to tell Jonny.

'Well that's amazing because our next activity is to make a miniature garden. We can make one for Bob so he can be around plants while he's inside the house. It'll be like his own little garden.

'Sounds good,' I said, 'how do we do it?'

Activity Number 8

Miniature Garden

Equipment

A plastic, foil or ceramic container

Soil

Small plants

Small pebbles

Twigs

Little toys

Method

Fill the container with soil.

Sketch a design showing what you want to go where..

Add pebbles, small plants, twigs and anything else you need to build your garden. We added a small mirror to make a pond.

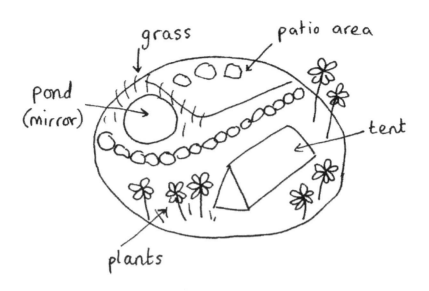

Half way through making it I went outside to tell Bob what we were doing. He came in and joined us. He even remembered there was a small stool shaped piece of plastic that came in a pizza box so he added that too.

We were really pleased with the miniature garden and me and Bob sat on the patio area. It felt exactly like we were sitting in real garden.

Bob seemed to forget all about being collected in two weeks and set about making a small tent out of a tea towel, so he could camp in the new garden.

As I lay in bed that night I began to think about Bob and the man in the purple cardigan. I thought about why Bob hadn't told us he had a name, and wondered will happen when the man comes to collect him?

The next morning, I raced downstairs and saw Bob sitting next to the tiny tent.

'It was brilliant sleeping in there,' he said smiling. 'I love this garden.

I climbed into the pot and sat on a pebble. Jonny came downstairs and gave us a marshmallow each for breakfast. (not a very healthy breakfast but it was a special occasion as we were celebrating Bob's first night camping in the tiny garden.)

Later that day there was a knock on the door. It was Jeremy Mothballs, 'hi everyone,' he said coming in, I've brought some droodles anyone want to see them?'

We all nodded eagerly and Jonny made him a cup of tea.

Activity Number 9

Picture Puzzle- Droodles

Jeremy spread out a number of pictures on the carpet and we all sat on the floor to have a look. 'A droodle is a combination of a doodle and a riddle. You have to look at a picture and guess what it is....

We all looked at the first one...

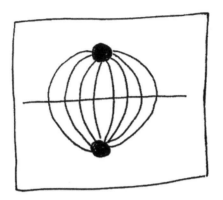

'No idea,' said Bob.

'Um, is it a pumpkin?' I asked.

'No, it's a spider standing on a mirror,' said Jeremy grinning. We all had another look.

'Of course,' said Jonny.

'Okay let's try some more,' said Jeremy putting four more down.

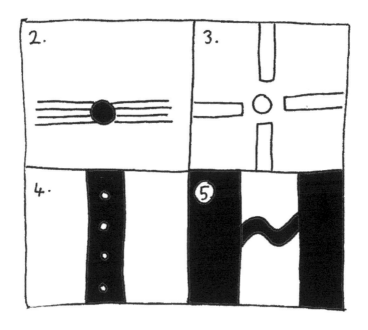

We looked at them for a long time.

'I Give up,' said Bob.

Okay, I'll give you the answers,' said Jeremy

2 – A spider doing the splits.

3 – Four elephants inspecting a grapefruit (from above).

4 – A watch strap in a box

5 – A black snake on a zebra crossing.

We all had a good laugh at number three.

'Do you want to try another four?' asked Jeremy.

'Yes, yes,' we said.

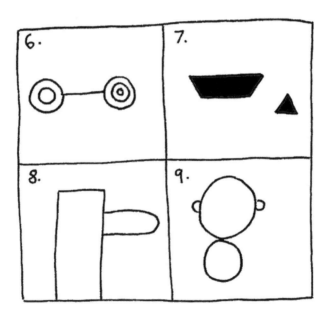

'Is number nine Eric Trum bending over?' said Bob. We had a look and I felt my cheeks flushing.

'Um no,' said Jeremy, 'I'll give you the answers.

6 – A man in a top hat frying an egg.

7 – A boat going to rescue a sinking witch.

8 – A trombone player in a cupboard.

9 – A bald man with bubble-gum (definitely not Eric Trum)

'These are brilliant', I said to Jeremy, 'have you got any more?'

'Yes, I've got another three,' he said, spreading them out.

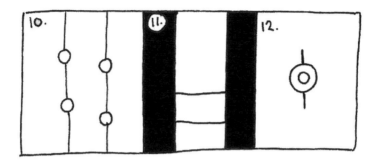

Answers

10 – A bear climbing the far side of a tree.

11 – A sausage dog passing a gap in a fence.

12 – A cowboy riding a bicycle.

'They were really good,' we said to Jeremy, and Jonny made him another cup of tea. After that Jeremy and Jonny went into the kitchen and looked at the postcard from Keith Kettle-Chaser.

'Oh no,' said Jeremy, 'I thought Bob was here forever.'

'Me too,' shouted Bob from the lounge.

We had some spaghetti and Jonny asked Jeremy if he wanted to be in a competition.

'I love competitions,' said Jeremy, 'what is it?'

'It's a sunflower growing competition,' said Jonny.

Activity Number 10

Sunflower Growing Competition

'I'll join in,' said Bob, 'as long as I can plant my sunflower in my new miniature garden.

'So how do we do it?' I asked. Jonny got some yogurt pots out of a cupboard.

'I'll show you,' he said.

Equipment

1 yogurt or plant pot per person

soil

some sunflower seeds

Method

1. *Poke a few holes in the bottom of your pot for drainage. (If you do this, make sure you keep your pot on a saucer.)*
2. *Fill your pot with soil, then make a hole in the soil with your finger, (or whole arm if you're a stick man).*
3. *drop a seed into the hole then cover it up with soil.*
4. *Water your seed.*

How it went for us

Bob decided to plant his seed in the miniature garden so he didn't have to add any soil. The rest of us filled our yogurt pots. It took me quite a long time because I used a tea spoon to shovel the soil in.

Once it was full we made our holes. I used my whole arm and actually found out I was stuck. It was rather embarrassing because my head was jammed against the soil and my bum was sticking out. **I WAS NOT AT ALL HAPPY ABOUT THIS.**

'Look at Eric's bum,' said Bob. I struggled to free my arm so that I could run behind something and hide but I couldn't move. 'It's enormous,' he carried on. The more I wiggled about trying to free my arm the more he laughed.

'Don't be mean to Eric,' said Jeremy.

'Oh, Eric doesn't mind,' said Bob.

'I do mind actually', I said, but no one heard

because I was face down in the soil.

After a lot of struggling and some help from Jonny I got out and we planted our seeds.

'Right, everyone is in charge of watering their own seed,' said Jonny, 'once the plant start growing you can put it in a bigger pot if you like, and when they flower, we'll measure them.'

'What will the winner get?' asked Bob.

'The winner will be allowed to have a ride on my remote-controlled spider,' said Jonny.

Me and Bob smiled, Jeremy frowned.

'Bye,' said Jeremy leaving with his yogurt pot tucked under his arm.

That evening we watched DaveHax on YouTube for twenty-two minutes before going to bed. Bob slept in the tent in the miniature garden again, which is an improvement on his old place behind the bin.

In the middle of the night I felt a tapping on my head. I opened my eyes and saw that it was Bob.

'What is it?' I asked.

'I've just had a thought,' If Keith Kettle-Chaser takes me away I won't be able to finish the sunflower growing competition,' he said.

'Well you could take it with you and pop back when it flowers?' I said.

'Maybe,' he said,' but what if Keith Kettle-Chaser lives miles away.

'I know,' I said, leaping out of my sock, 'let's google him and see if we can find out where he lives?'

Bob started jumping up and down very fast. We both ran into the kitchen where Jonny had left the laptop.

I typed in 'Keith Kettle-Chaser' and we found a website all about him. It turned out he was an artist and photographer. His work was very strange but we recognized some of the places in his photographs and decided he must live nearby.

'I might see if he'll let me stay with you,' said Bob, 'after all he never played with me.'

'Good plan,' I said.

Bob started yawning. 'I think we'd better both go back to sleep,' he said, 'and by the way, sorry about laughing at your bum.'

'Thank you,' I said before racing back upstairs and diving back into my sock which was still warm.

The next morning, I woke Jonny and told him about the Keith Kettle-Chaser website. He had a look and said he thought it was quite good.

There was a knock on the door. Jonny went to open it but there was no one around, just an envelope left on the door mat. Inside was a card with a deflated balloon and a pin taped onto it.

'I wonder what this is for?' said Jonny holding up the pin.

'I'm not sure but let's blow the balloon up and play keep the balloon in the air,' I said.

Jonny started blowing, as it got bigger he realised there was something inside it. It looked like a folded piece of paper.

'I know,' I said, 'the pin is to pop it, so we can get the message out.'

Jonny looked very excited. 'I'm scared to pop it though, I don't like bangs.' He handed me the pin but I didn't want to do it either so we called Bob through. Luckily Bob jumped straight onto it with the pin in his hand and it popped straight away. The piece of paper fell to the floor and Bob unfolded it.

Dear Jonny, Eric and Bob,

You are invited to a jokes night at my house on Friday at six o'clock.

Yours sincerely Jeremy Mothballs.

'What's a joke night?' asked Bob.

'Well what usually happens is that we all go to Jeremy's and take it in turns to tell some jokes.'

Bob nodded, 'well I prefer practical jokes so I might do those instead,' he said.

After that we all watered our sunflowers then disappeared into different corners of the house to work on our jokes.

A bit later on Bob said he was going to make some practical jokes and needed to spend a long time in the kitchen on his own. Jonny and I stayed in the lounge.

Bob's Secret Activity

Activity Number 11

Salt Dough Jokes

Hello, Bob here I'm going to tell you about my salt dough jokes. I made a fake mouse to put in Jonny's shoe, a fake poo to put on one of the cushions and something else that is going to be a BIG surprise.

Here's the salt dough recipe. (make sure an adult helps as the oven is hot.)

Ingredients

1 cup of salt

1 cup of water

2 cups of flour

method

1. *Put the flour and salt in a bowl then add the water slowly until it's a nice doughy consistency. (you may not need all the water)*
2. *Make the shapes you want.*
3. *Bake them at 180C until hard (baking time depends on the thickness of the dough. mine took about an hour.)*
4. *Once dry you can paint them.*

Tip tip

As well as mice and poo you could also make

fake food but make sure no one accidentally eats it.

I put the finished items into a paper bag and hid them ready to take to the party on Friday.

Activity Number 12

Jeremy Mothball's Joke Night

Hello, I'm back, yes, it's me Eric. I'll prove it's me by showing you a picture. There you go. (I hope you looked at my nice shiny recorder rather than my 'you know what.')

I found this recorder in a cupboard and have been learning to play for an hour. I can only reach the top hole though so can only play two notes which Jonny is finding rather annoying. Anyway, my new hobby has given me the brilliant idea of telling musical jokes.

We all gathered our jokes together and set off at five to six.

Jeremy led us all into his house and we sat on the sofa. Suddenly Jeremy jumped up, 'what's that?' he yelled. He was pointing at a rather disturbing looking brown lump, 'Oh my goodness, it's a poo!' We all leapt out of our seats and Jeremy ran off to get some tissues.

'HA HA PRANKED,' shouted Bob picking up the fake poo.

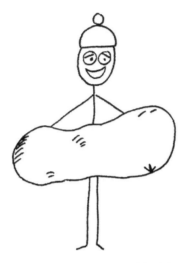

We all had a look at it and decided it was quite a good joke.

After that it was time for me to tell my jokes so I stood on the wooden box stage. I was nervous but took a deep breath and began.

1. Which Musical instrument is found in the bathroom? – **A tuba toothpaste**.

2. Why is a piano hard to open? – **because the keys are on the inside.**
3. What type of music are balloons scared of? – **Pop music** (my best joke).
4. What makes music on your head? – **A headband.**
5. What stops Jazz musicians from floating off into space? – **Groovity.**

Everyone clapped and I took a bow. Then I saw Bob running out of the room. He was gone for a couple of minutes before running back in with something tied onto him. It was a FAKE BUM!!!!

I stared in horror as he started dancing around saying my name is Eric Trum.' Jonny picked him up and took him into the hall. A few minutes later he came back in without the bum. 'Sorry Eric,' he mumbled before sitting back down. 'I thought it would be funny.'

'Well it wasn't funny,' said Jeremy.

Next it was time for Jeremy's jokes. He got on the stage....

1. *Today a man knocked on my door and asked for a small donation toward the local swimming pool,* **so I gave him a glass of water.**

2. I changed my password to 'incorrect,' so whenever I forget what it is, the computer will say '**your password is incorrect**.' (Good one Jeremy.)
3. It you're not supposed to eat at night, **why is there a light bulb in the fridge**?
4. **Turtles think frogs are homeless**.
5. I can't believe I got fired from my job in the calendar factory**, all I did was take a day off.**
6. The sad thing about tennis is that however good I get, **I'll never be as good as a wall**.

We were all in hysterics by the end. Bob and I were rolling around on the floor and the whole fake bottom thing had been forgotten.

'So just Jonny left to go,' said Jeremy. Jonny looked a bit concerned as he left the room to get ready.

'I only have one joke but I think it'll be enough said Jonny from the hallway.' We all waited eagerly. There were some banging noises then Jonny came back in dragging a rocking chair behind him. He sat on it and put some roller-skates on. He began to rock, his skates rolling backward and forward as he went.

We all looked at him wondering what was going on.

'Why am I sitting in this rocking chair with roller-skates on?' he asked.

We all shook our heads, 'no idea,' said Jeremy.

'Because I want to **Rock and Roll**,' he said, 'I want to rock and roll! Get it?'

'Oh Yes, I get it,' said Jeremy, clapping. Jonny

smiled as he took his skates off.

Just as we were putting our shoes on to leave Jonny started screaming then he jumped into Jeremy's arms.

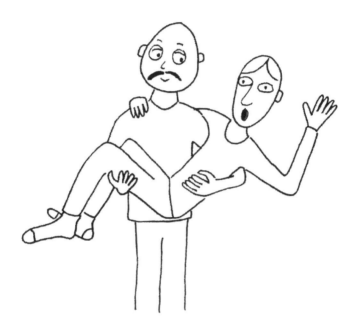

We had a look and saw that there was a little mouse peeking out of his shoe.

'Just my last little joke,' said Bob getting the mouse out.

'Good one,' we all said, patting him on the back. We went home and went to bed, Bob sleeping in the tent in the miniature garden.

The next day we went back onto the computer and looked at Keith Kettle-Chasers website again. There were some new drawings he'd done and a picture of him in a purple cardigan.

'Does he always wear that?' I asked Bob.

'He has several different purple cardigans,' said Bob, 'I've never seen him not wearing one.'

'I quite like them, I might get a purple cardigan,' said Jonny.

'When Keith comes to collect me, I'm going to hide,' said Bob.

'Don't worry,' said Jonny, 'I'll talk to Keith and see if you can live here, or at least have regular visits.'

Bob nodded and Jonny got a cucumber out of the fridge. We had a nice spa day where we lay in baths with pieces of cucumber on our faces. It was actually quite relaxing and took my mind off the worry of what might happen when Keith Kettle-Chaser turns up.

In the evening, Jeremy came around and we all sat at the kitchen table ready to play a game. There were four pencils and four long thin pieces of paper. 'This is quite exciting,' said Jeremy, 'what's the game?'

Activity Number 13

Picture Consequences

We each picked up the piece of paper in front of us and Jonny told us to fold it in half then in half again so there would be three fold lines when we unfolded it…. like this.

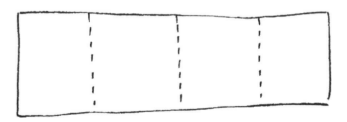

'Right,' said Jonny, 'we all have to secretly draw a head in the first section, and make sure the neck shows just beyond the crease.

I drew a head. This is what mine looked like.

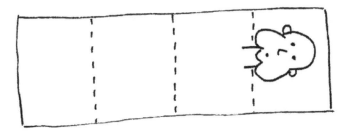

Next we had to fold the paper back so that the heads were hidden with just the neck showing, we passed the pieces of paper to the person on our left.

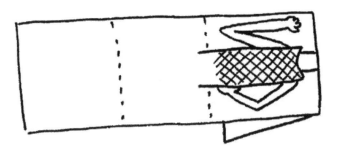

'Next draw the body,' said Jonny, 'make sure a bit of the body goes over the crease.'

Then we folded the bit we'd drawn on down and passed it on. The next thing was the legs down to the knees and the last one was the lower legs and feet. Once we'd finished we passed them along one more time before opening them.

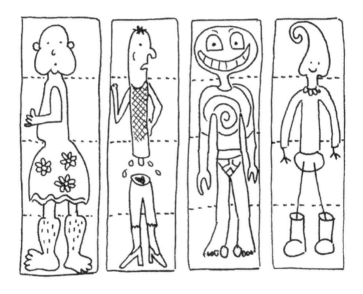

This is what they looked like. I laughed and laughed until I fell over.

'That is such a good game,' said Jeremy before making us all a cup (or thimbleful) of tea.

Once Jeremy had gone home Jonny, Bob and I sat under a blanket and watched a TV show about holidays.

'We've not been on holiday for a while,' I said to Jonny.

'That's true, shall we go on one tomorrow?'

Me and Bob both nodded and it was agreed that we would go away the very next day.

We got up early and Jonny threw a sleeping bag into the back of his funny red van. He also packed some warm socks to be sleeping bags for the smaller travellers

Jonny got into the driving seat and Bob and I sat on the dash board looking out of the window. 'So where are we going?' asked Bob.

'I don't know,' said Jonny, 'but I'll know it when I see it.' As we set off Bob began singing a song which went like this.

I'm a travelling stick man

Going on my holiday

I've packed my sock and my thimble

Things are going my way.

I'll be relaxing

Somewhere fun

And I'll be hanging out

with the one with a big bum.

I stared straight ahead pretending I hadn't heard.

'A game,' said Jonny, 'let's play a travel game.'

Activity number 14

Car Snooker

Jonny explained the rules to us. Here they are.

The rules of car snooker

Each player has five minutes to spot different coloured cars, vans or lorries in colour order. Here is the order we decided on....

Red - 1 point

Yellow - 2 points

Green – 3 points

Brown – 4 points

Blue – 5 points

Pink – 6 points

Black – 7 points

If you get through all the colours you can start going through the list again, starting with red. For each one you spot you get the points associated with that colour.

Jonny had already written all the colours out on bits of paper so we just had to tick them off.

It was decided that Bob was going to go first as he was by far the most excited and couldn't stop wriggling around. I set the timer on Jonny's phone to five minutes and he started looking.

He saw a red car almost straight away and ticked it off, we had to wait quite a long time for a yellow vehicle but luckily a Morrison lorry went past which was half yellow. There was then a green car followed by a van that was probably black but it was so muddy we said it could pass as brown. Then the timer went off.

We counted up the points and Bob had scored 10 points.

'Right Eric, it's your go,' said Bob passing me the pencil. He set the timer off and I eagerly looked for a red vehicle. Luckily there was a red post van so I ticked that off. I began looking for a yellow car but there were none! Where are all the yellow vehicles????

I kept glancing at the timer going down and I began to get worried. Luckily, I saw a motorway maintenance truck that was mostly yellow so I ticked that off. Phew!!

I got green, brown (muddy) and blue but there didn't seem to be a pink car anywhere. Still I managed to get 15 points so I was the winner.

'I think we should get rid of the pink colour, it's too hard,' I said. Luckily Jonny agreed and we crossed it off the list. We played the game seventeen more times (without the pink) and it was really fun.

Suddenly Jonny took a sharp left turn and we nearly fell off the dash board.

'What's going on?' said Bob, picking himself up.

'We've arrived,' said Jonny as we wobbled along a pebbly road. We carried on through some trees and saw the beach. Bob stared open mouthed.

'What is it?' he asked, looking at the water.

'Have you never seen the sea before?' asked Jonny.'

'No,' said Bob, 'it's amazing.

We parked up the van and ran down onto the beach. We sat on pebbles overlooking the sea. It sparkled with orange flecks as the sun set. 'I love it here,' I said as I breathed in the salty air.

'I think it's time for a little bonfire and some food', said Jonny. Bob and I rushed off to help find sticks to burn while Jonny went back to the van. We ate our hardboiled egg and jam sandwiches and started the fire.

'We're going to make smores for pudding,' said Jonny. He got marshmallows, digestive biscuits and a bar of chocolate out of his bag.

Activity Number 15

Camp Fire Smores

Ingredients

Digestive Biscuits

Marshmallows

Chocolate

Method

1. *Put a piece of chocolate on top of one of the digestive biscuits.*
2. *Put a marshmallow on a stick and roast it over the fire until it is very soft.*
3. *Put the roasted marshmallow on top of the chocolate*
4. *Put another digestive on top to make a sandwich*

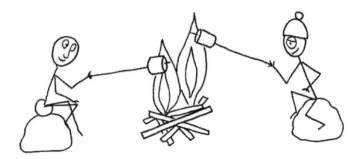

It was good fun cooking the marshmallows, although we had to find rather long sticks to make sure we weren't too near the fire. The smores were absolutely delicious. Because we are small we used mini marshmallows and quarter pieces of digestives and it all worked out beautifully.

We sat on pebbles feeling very full and watched the fire for quite a while.

'You know what Jonny,' said Bob, 'you're not too bad, for a human.'

'Well you're a very nice stick man,' said Jonny.

'I'm worried about Keith Kettle-Chaser, life with him won't be as good.'

'I'll talk to him,' said Jonny.

The sun went down and the fire went out. It was very dark and we could see hundreds of stars in the sky. We lay on the beach watching them for a while then got into the back of the van and went to sleep.

The next morning Bob and I ran down to the beach. I dug a small hole and put my bottom in it. Suddenly I looked exactly like a normal stickman. Bob frowned. 'I think I prefer you with the big bum actually,' he said, 'you look too normal without it.'

I tried to hide my smile.

'Look,' I said, pointing at a figure running towards us. It was Jonny carrying a large beach ball and two small water pistols. I tried to jump up but was jammed in the sand so Bob dug me out and we stood up.

'What have you got?' asked Bob.

'The equipment for a game of squirt ball,' said Jonny handing us each a water pistol

Activity Number 16

Squirt Ball

We immediately ran to the sea and filled up our pistols. I got absolutely soaked in the process so I rolled on Jonny's towel for a bit. When I got up Bob squirted me with the water. 'Nooooooooo, it's cold,' I yelled.

'Right let's play squirt ball,' said Jonny.

How to play

Draw a dot and two parallel lines in the sand like this. Each person is assigned a line.

Put a beach ball on the dot. Each player stands next to their line with a full water pistol. Once the referee says go the players run in and try and get the ball to roll over the other person's line by squiring water at it. No physical touching of the ball is allowed, it has to be moved by squirt power alone! If you run out of water you can go back to the sea or to a bucket to refill.

Top Tips

This game doesn't work well if it's very windy.

You can play this in the garden by using chalk, string or masking tape instead of lines in the sand.

How it went for us

We started squirting away and the ball actually began to move. Unfortunately, the ball was bigger than me and, as it rolled, I got stuck underneath and ended up being pressed into the sand.

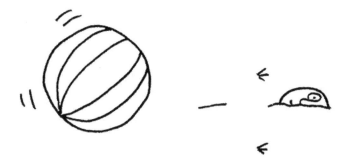

I got up and brushed myself down. Luckily Jonny had a smaller ball in his bag and we tried again with that. This worked much better for us and I won the first game. Bob won the second and third games and I won the fourth game so it was sort of a draw. To celebrate, we tried to balance on top of the ball until it was lunchtime.

Alternative version of the Squirt Game

The players can work as a team and squirt together to get the ball to roll over a line drawn some distance along the beach.

Activity Number 17

Build a Sand Man

After we'd eaten our jam sushi rolls for lunch we decided to build sandmen. Bob and I worked together and used our teaspoons to dig up enough sand to make a stick man figure in the sand. We had a long debate about whether it should have a big bum or not and in the end decided it should. We made eyes and a mouth out of pebbles and once we'd finished it looked really good.

Jonny made his own sand man which he said

represented his inner self.

That evening we had another bonfire and more smores. Jonny had some bubble liquid so, after tea, we played pop the bubbles on the beach then we decided to try swimming in the sea. It was absolutely freezing and we only got in up to our waists (but at least my 'you know what' was hidden.)

'Look at that,' said Bob pointing at something. We all had a look, it was like a whitish blob of jelly with long ribbons hanging off it.

'It's a jellyfish,' said Jonny, 'they can sting you so

be careful.'

'It's the best thing I've ever seen,' said Bob quickly leaving the water.

We watched the sky turn red as the sun set before climbing into the back of the van. 'That was my best day ever,' said Bob as we snuggled into our sleeping socks.

The next day we all piled into the front of the van and headed for home. We played a few rounds of car snooker and after that we played the alphabet name game, where you have to think of a girl's name for every letter of the alphabet.

Eventually we pulled up at 41 Brooklands Avenue and ran in. There was a postcard on the doormat. It was from Keith Kettle-Chaser! 'What does it say? What does it say?' said Bob.

Jonny read it out. 'I will be coming to see my dear Ludwig on Monday.'

'That's you Bob,' I said, 'he's coming to get you!'

Bob looked worried. 'That's just three days away,' he said. We opened the laptop and had a look at Keith Kettle-Chasers blog. He'd put some photos of sand sculptures on there.

'Oh look, he likes playing with sand too,' I said. But Bob had already climbed into his miniature garden and crawled into his tea towel tent.

Bob refused to come out of his tent the next day but Jonny had an idea. 'Let's make some gingerbread men, the delicious smell is sure to lure him out.'

I nodded eagerly.

Activity Number 18

Gingerbread Men

'This is the most complicated recipe we've ever done,' said Jonny, 'but it's an emergency, we have to get Bob out.'

He started getting all the ingredients out of the cupboard.

Ingredients

350g plain flour, plus extra for rolling out

> *1 tsp bicarbonate of soda*
> *2 tsp ground ginger*
> *1 tsp ground cinnamon*
> *125g butter*
> *175g light soft brown sugar*
> *4 tbsp. golden syrup*

1 egg

You will also need a gingerbread man cutter, but if you don't have one you can make your own shapes out of the dough instead.

Method

1. *Mix together the flour, bicarbonate of soda, ginger and cinnamon and pour into a bowl. Add the butter and twiddle it between your fingers until the mix looks like breadcrumbs. Stir in the sugar.*
2. *Lightly beat the egg and golden syrup together with a fork, add to the bowl and mix and squeeze it all together until it becomes a lump. Tip the dough out, knead briefly until smooth, wrap in cling film and leave in the fridge for 15 minutes.*
3. *Preheat the oven to 180C/350F/Gas 4. Line two baking trays with greaseproof paper.*
4. *Roll the dough out to a 0.5cm thickness on a lightly floured surface and use cutters to cut out the shapes. Place on the baking tray, leaving a gap between them and bake for 12-15 minutes (or until light golden brown.)*

How it went for us

I had to have a very good wash under the tap because Jonny told me that I would be going into the mixture and that's exactly what I did. Once the ingredients were in the bowl I dived in and rolled around until everything started mixing together. It took a long time and Jonny helped too by rubbing the mixture between his fingers. It was rather like swimming in breadcrumbs at one stage.

We rolled out the dough and cut out gingerbread men shapes before putting them in the oven. After a few minutes the most yumolicious smell started wafting through the house.

'What's that smell?' said a voice from inside a tea towel tent.

'Yummy biscuits,' said Jonny, come and help us decorate them. Bob came through and we all waited for them to be ready. When the timer went off, Jonny took them out and put them on a wire tray to cool.

Once they were cool Jonny got a black icing pen and drew stick men shapes in the middle of some of them like this….

'Can I try one?' asked Bob. Jonny nodded and broke off an arm for me and an arm for Bob then ate the rest himself.

'Now we'll save the rest in case we have any visitors next week,' said Jonny, I knew he meant Keith Kettle-Chaser but Bob didn't seem to realize and was very busy eating his biscuit. Jonny took two gingerbread men and decorated them, adding eyes, a smiley mouth and purple icing cardigans. He hid them away before Bob noticed.

That afternoon Bob and I watched a film called

'Nine Lives,' about a man who turned into a cat, while Jonny went to the craft shop to get some googley eyes and ribbons for a craft activity.

'I'm home, I'm home,' he called later as he rushed in carrying a craft shop bag. 'Remember how you liked that jellyfish we saw at the beach? Well I've got everything we need to make out own fantastic jellyfishes tomorrow!'

'Sounds brilliant,' said Bob.

Once Bob had gone into his tent, Jonny and I went upstairs.

'I'm worried about Bob leaving,' I said, 'I quite like having him around now.'

'I know, but hopefully we can come to some arrangement with Keith Kettle-Chaser.'

I didn't sleep well that night, I kept tossing and turning until my sock was all twisted up.

Activity Number 19

Jellyfish

Jeremy Mothballs doesn't work on a Sunday so he came around to make Jellyfish with us.

What you need

1. *Containers to use as the body. You can use yogurt pots, dome lids from takeaway drinks or the bottom of bottles.*
2. *Ribbons to use as tentacles. (Jonny got silver ones) If you don't have any, you can cut a*

plastic bag into strips.

3. *Googley eyes (or permanent pen to draw eyes)*
4. *Cotton or string to hang the jelly fish up.*

Method

1. *If you are using a bottle, cut the bottom off to be the body.*
2. *Punch holes in the body using a hole punch (or ask a grown up to help you melt holes in using a heated metal skewer.)*
3. *Tie pieces of ribbon through the holes, leaving long trailing tentacles.*
4. *Glue or draw eyes onto the face, add a mouth if you like.*
5. *Hang your finished jellyfish from the ceiling.*

We made one each and hung them up around the kitchen. Here is what mine looked like.

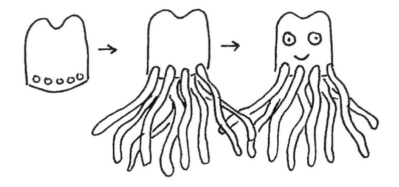

As we looked at them Jonny got some tubs of jelly out of the fridge.

'Yes,' I shouted, 'I love jellyfish… and jelly.'

As a treat, Jonny let Bob and me go into jelly pots after tea and it was sooooo fun.

'Hey, what's red, flies and wobbles at the same time?' said Jonny.

'I don't know,' I said, flicking a piece of jelly off my head.

'A jelly-copter,' said Jonny.

I laughed politely and Bob disappeared into his Jelly pot.

'I can't believe this is Bob's last day,' said Jeremy quietly.

'I know,' said Jonny, 'But don't talk about it or it

might upset him.'

'What might upset me?' said Bob, bobbing back up.

'Um nothing,' said Jeremy going red.

'Is it about tomorrow?' said Bob.

'Don't worry about tomorrow,' said Jonny, 'I'll try and sort it all out, and if you do go back home, you can take your garden and tent with you.'

Bob suddenly started crying. We all stood in shock not knowing what to say. 'But this is my home now,' he sobbed.

I put my jelly covered hand on his.

Later that day we sat on the back doorstep looking over the garden. 'I've got a great game to play', said Jonny. It's called sellotape marbles, who's in?'

We all nodded, even Bob who probably wanted to take his mind off his worries.

Activity Number 20

Sellotape marbles

Ingredients

Double sided sellotape

Marbles

Chalk or string to mark a start line.

How to play

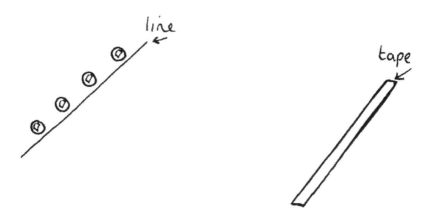

1. Find a place to play. This game is best played on a hard surface outside (as the double sided

sellotape could damage inside surfaces.)

2. Stick a long piece of double sided tape to the floor and draw a line with chalk about 30cm away from it.

3. Everyone crouches behind the line with their marble. Try to roll the marble so it sticks to the tape. If you roll it too hard, it just goes over it, if you roll it too softly it doesn't reach it.

We played it on our little patio area in the (real) garden and it was actually great fun.

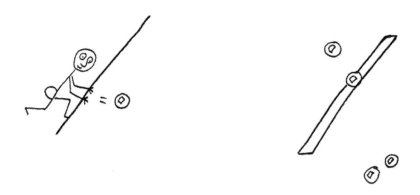

Bob seemed to forget all about being collected and had about fifty goes.

As Jeremy left he gave Bob a big hug, 'I hope to see you very soon,' he said before rushing home rubbing his eyes.

We all went inside and sat in silence.

I woke early the next day, Jonny was vacuuming the whole house and trying to make everything as tidy as possible. Bob was still in his tent so, once the house was tidy, Jonny and I made a few more jellyfish to hang around the kitchen.

Bob still wasn't up at lunchtime and we knew Keith Kettle-Chaser was coming after lunch so I was sent in to wake him up. I crawled into the tea towel tent and was shocked to find he wasn't there!

I ran out and told Jonny. 'Oh no,' said Jonny as he began running around looking for him. Eventually we found him hiding in a tree in the garden. Just then the doorbell rang.

'Just see what happens,' I said.

Bob linked my arm and was shaking slightly as he came back into the house.

There in the kitchen was Keith Kettle-Chaser. He was tall and thin with a long purple cardigan on. He stroked his chin as Jonny introduced himself.

'I'm a big fan of your books Eric,' said Keith.

'Thank you, 'I said.

Then he saw Bob, 'Ludwig,' he shouted.

'Um, I'm called Bob now,' said Bob.

'Really?' he looked at Jonny who nodded. We all sat down for a cup of tea.

'I love the jellyfish,' said Keith looking at the models hanging around the kitchen.

'I made the one with just one eye,' said Bob.

'I love that one most,' said Keith and Bob smiled.

After a cup of tea, (and a purple cardigan wearing gingerbread man), Bob offered to show Keith around the house. He showed him the miniature garden with the tea towel tent and all the different rooms. He even had a game of Sellotape marbles with him in the garden.

'So how come Bob thought humans and stick men shouldn't hang out together?' Jonny asked Keith when he came back in.

'Well,' said Keith, 'When Bob started talking I thought I must be imagining it. I mean it seemed very unlikely that a stick man could be alive. I was worried I was losing my mind so I tried to keep away from him.'

'I see,' said Jonny.

'I'd read your books but I thought you'd just made Eric up. I actually thought your book had put funny ideas into my head.'

'So how come you posted Bob to us?'

'It was just in case it was true,' said Keith, putting his head in his hands, 'I've been such a fool, I should have looked after him better.' He turned to Bob, 'I'm sorry, life will be good from now on, I promise.'

'But I like it here,' said Bob.

'You can help me with my art,' said Keith, 'judging by your jelly fish, you're very good at making things.'

Bob beamed, 'Oh, thank you.'

'you can even sleep in my room,' said Keith.

'But I still want to see Eric and Jonny.'

'We can visit, we only live ten minutes away.'

'Can you visit every weekend?' I asked.

Keith nodded.

'Can I take the miniature garden and tent with me?' said Bob.

Keith looked at Jonny who nodded and said yes.

Jonny and I watched as they drove away. It was very quiet. I'd forgotten what it was like when it was just us two.

'Let's look for some new things to do,' I said climbing onto Jonny's shoulder. 'We need to keep busy.'

The next Saturday Bob and Keith came to visit.

'How's it going' asked Jonny.

'It's great,' said Keith, 'we've been doing art every day.'

'I love it,' said Bob, 'and I've got lots of ideas for weekend activities we can all do together,' he said.

They came to visit most weekends after that, then one weekend a few months later Keith came in carrying the miniature garden. In the middle of it was a large sunflower.

'Remember the sunflower competition?' asked Bob. I looked at Jonny and Jonny looked at me, we'd forgotten all about it and our sunflowers had died.

Later that day Jeremy came to see us. He was carrying a pot with a sunflower in it too. We measured the two sunflowers and Bob was the winner. 'Yay,' said Bob climbing to the top of the stem, 'life is good.'

'Can you remember the prize for having the tallest sunflower?' asked Jonny.

'No,' said Bob.

'You get a ride on my remote-controlled spider!'

'YIPPEE,' said Bob. He climbed down the flower as Jonny went to get it.

'Right, time for your ride.'

'Wahoo,' said Bob, 'come on Eric, there's room for you too.'

We rode the spider for two hours and were very happy.

Well that's the end for now. But we'll be back again soon with more fun ideas.

Have you read our other books?

Also available from Half Man Half Octopus…

Printed in Great Britain
by Amazon